The GINGERBREAD MAN LOOSE at CHRISTMAS

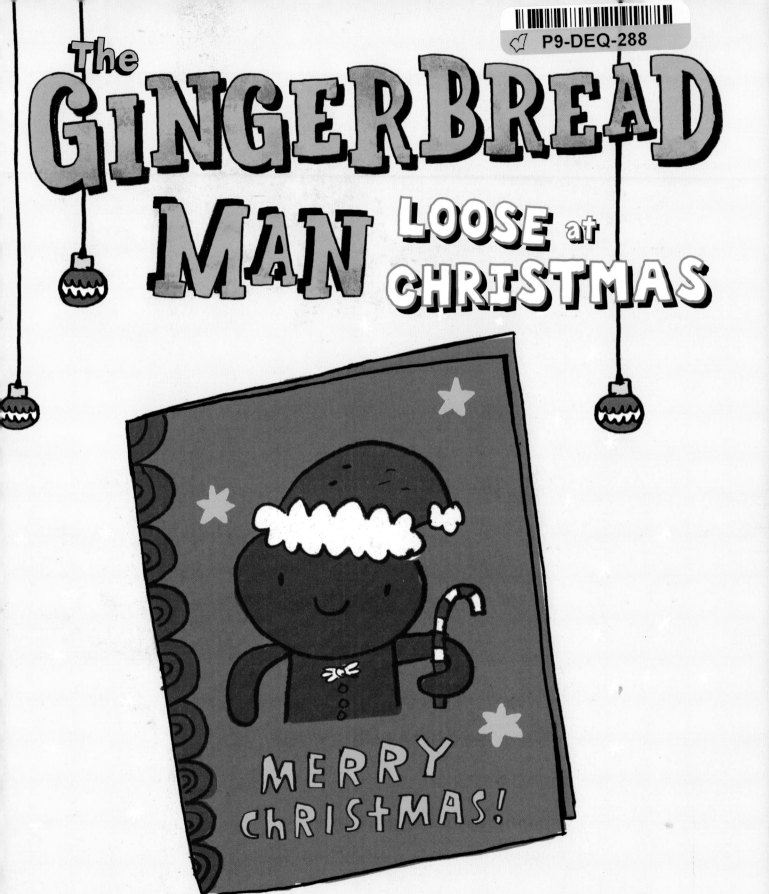

MERRY CHRISTMAS!

Laura Murray · illustrated by **Mike Lowery**

SCHOLASTIC INC.

To my amazing editor, Susan,
and my awesome agent, Marietta—
thank you for your insight, support,
and guidance. You have given me
the gift of a dream come true.
—L.M.

For my favorite people,
Katrin and Allister.
—M.L.

ISBN 978-1-338-11396-9

Text copyright © 2015 by Laura Murray. Illustrations copyright © 2015 by Mike Lowery.
All rights reserved. Published by Scholastic Inc., 557 Broadway, New York, NY 10012,
by arrangement with G. P. Putnam's Sons, an imprint of Penguin Young Readers Group,
a division of Penguin Random House LLC. SCHOLASTIC and associated logos are trademarks
and/or registered trademarks of Scholastic Inc.

12 11 10 9 8 7 6 5 4 3 2   16 17 18 19 20 21

Printed in the U.S.A.   40

First Scholastic printing, November 2016

Design by Ryan Thomann
Text set in Bokka and Dr. Eric, with a bit of hand-lettering
The illustrations were rendered with pencil, traditional screen printing, and digital color.

One white snowy morning, I popped from my bed.

My teacher was calling,

WAKE UP, SLEEPYHEAD!

The classroom was decked out in holiday **lights**.
They **twinkled** and **sparkled** in reds, greens, and **whites**.

I'LL **THINK** OF A **PRESENT.**
I KNOW THAT I CAN!
I WANT TO GIVE, TOO. I'M THE
GINGERBREAD MAN!

Some children made **CARDS,**

and others baked **TREATS.**

A few practiced **singing** with jingle-bell **BEATS.**

I wanted my **present** to be a **surprise.**
I thought and I thought,
then I **grabbed** my **supplies.**

I knew **JUST** the person I'd give **this** gift to,

so I made something **special**

with **glitter** and **glue.**

The town was so **merry**! The storefronts **aglow**.
Each window was **frosted** with white icy **snow**.

We stopped a **police lady**, sang her a **SONG**.
She **smiled** really big as she waved us **along**.

Next came a **garbage man** picking up **trash**,
so we dropped off some goodies to **stash** on his **dash**.

We raced to the

DENTIST,

the

GROCER,

the **VET**–
delivering **cheer**
to each neighbor
we **met.**

THANK YOU!

They all seemed so
HAPPY
and very
SURPRISED!

They gave us
BEAR HUGS,

and a few
even **cried.**

I patted my pocket, then started to fret.

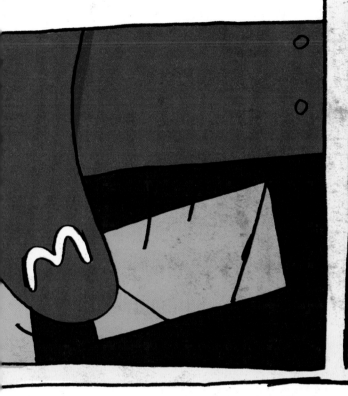

I STILL HAVE MY PRESENT . . . I CAN'T GO BACK YET.

But the class didn't **hear** me. The wind was too **loud**. They all headed **back** through the holiday **crowd**.

I MUST FIND THE NEIGHBOR
I MADE MY GIFT FOR.
SHE HELPED MY CLASS MAKE ME.
OH, WHERE IS HER STORE?

The sidewalks were slick as I tripped and then tumbled.
I noticed my feet were all mushy and crumbled.

GULP!

My icing was dripping. My legs were just DOUGH. I had to get out of this wet, squishy SNOW!

I'VE COME TO SAY THANKS FOR YOUR SWEET RECIPE. WITHOUT IT, MY CLASS WOULD'VE NEVER MADE ME.

I HAVE SOMETHING FOR YOU— MY VERY BEST CARD. I USED LOTS OF GLITTER AND WORKED REALLY HARD.

MERRY CHRISTMAS!

Our teacher looked **puzzled**, but curious too.

WE HAVE ONE MORE PRESENT— A **POEM** JUST FOR **YOU!**

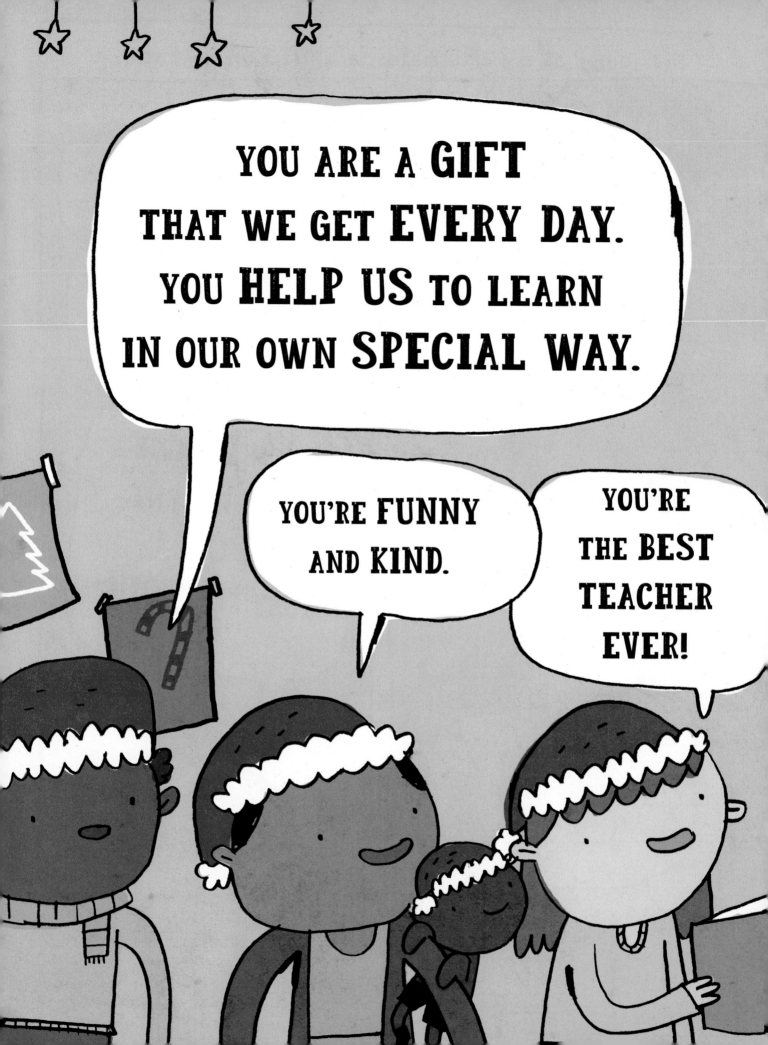

Our teacher **bent down**, and she **gathered us in**
with a **warmhearted hug** and a **very big grin**.

My **classmates** grinned, too.
We had **pulled off our plan!**